Front cover designed by
Ida Bennett

Illustrations by Ophelia Hayward

These things we take for granted,
One day we will see,
That everything once planted,
Will gradually cease to be.

- Tilia Cordata

The Umbolo Valley

by Ben Hayward

Chapter 1

The sun rose slowly above the horizon and cast its warm rays over the Umbolo Valley. A light wind blew down the gentle slopes, rustling the tall grasses as it flowed between them. A low rumbling could be heard in the distance and soon the sound grew nearer. A bus packed full of tourists rolled up one side of a hill and then down slowly into the valley.

The driver was accompanied by a guide with a microphone in his hand announcing himself to his captive audience.

'Good morning ladies and gentlemen,' he said, 'and welcome to the Umbolo Valley safari adventure. Hopefully, this morning you will be able to see some of the wildlife that this country has to offer. So, keep your eyes peeled and let me know if you spot something before I do.'

The bus trundled down a well-worn dirt track, deeper into the valley, the tourists with their faces pressed up against the glass of the window looking out for the slightest movement of anything. They slowed down when they reached an area where the grass was slightly longer and the guide began looking around in all directions.

'Ah,' he said, 'ladies and gentlemen, if you look to your right, you may catch a glimpse of one of the two lions we know of in this area.'

All eyes were now pinned on the lion that was gently making its way towards an unsuspecting wildebeest not too far away. The lion was crouched slightly, stalking its prey and getting closer and closer to its target.

The tourists started to squeal in excitement at the hunt they were about to see.

'This is a female lion,' the guide said quietly over his microphone, 'as is the case when it comes to the hunting. The *male lion will not be far away and will be expecting her to return with a meal for him shortly. Wildebeest are a common food for lions, along with zebra and antelope but they are capable of catching pretty much anything out here. She is not far from pouncing on this wildebeest now so keep watching.'*

The lion took three more steps then sprung out of the air with great speed and agility. But surprisingly, she missed the wildebeest which turned and began to run.

'How did she miss that?' someone on the bus said.

The lion however did not give up and began to give chase. The tourists were in for a real show now.

The wildebeest was quick and started to run towards the bus with the lion just behind. The pursuit flew right in front of the bus and off to the opposite side of the valley. The sudden rush of tourists from one set of windows to the other caused the bus to rock unsteadily. They were just in time to see both animals disappear in a tumble into the long grass.

'I can't see what's happening,' one man said. 'Did she get it?'

'Most likely,' said the guide. 'Now let's move on further down the valley and see what else we can find.'

The bus moved on as the passengers sat themselves back in their seats but it wasn't long before one of them had spotted something else.

'Look over there,' said a woman. 'What are those?'
The guide looked where the woman was pointing as the bus came to a stop again.

Three ostriches stood under the shade of an umbrella tree. Two of them had their heads buried in the ground whilst the third was pecking at the bark of the tree, unaware of the long, black length uncoiling behind its head.

'Here we have three ostriches which have been resting here over night,' said the guide. 'One has woken and disturbed the black spitting cobra that was sleeping in the tree. This ostrich, I think is about to find out how the cobra got its name!"

Just as he finished his sentence the cobra raised its head. Suddenly aware of its presence, the ostrich turned towards the cobra and received an eye full of snake spit. The ostrich squawked in surprise and began to run around frantically in circles. All the tourists began laughing and it took them a few moments to calm down.

'Now,' the guide started again, 'if you look back towards the Umbrella tree you can see the cranes moving about in the tops of the tree. They have to be ready to fly in case of an attack from their number one predator – the eagle.'

The tourists looked on as four cranes shuffled about on the branches. Suddenly a large, dark shadow moved across the sky. The eagle was a blur as it swept in for the attack. Only a few white feathers were left in the air where before a crane had stood.

The eagle had left with its prey, disappearing as swiftly as it had come in.

Now the tourists were looking, they could see the wildlife of the Umbolo Valley everywhere. There were hares chasing each other over the short grass of the slopes and a mongoose poked its head out from its burrow to catch some early morning sunshine. A baboon family were gently swinging from the branches of another umbrella tree. The guide also pointed out an aardvark and a porcupine that were foraging amongst the low shrubs in search of some breakfast.
The tourists soaked up the scene for a few more minutes before the bus started to move on down the valley again.

'We are now heading down towards the Umbolo Lake where we should find a different assortment of animals.' said the guide. 'There should be one or two crocodiles, maybe a few warthogs, some flamingos and on rare occasions, a black rhino uses the lake. We would be incredibly lucky to see the rhino though so don't get your hopes up too much.'

The bus followed the dirt track road down the side of a small stream that was one of many tributaries flowing into the lake and eventually, they came to the edge of the water. From their position, they could see across much of the lake and the guide began to point out some of the wildlife.

'Over here on the right we have some of the warthogs. There are also crocodiles skulking in the water. I don't think the warthogs know they are there because if they did, they wouldn't be so close. We'll hang around for a while and see if anything happens.'

The tourists focused their attention on the crocodiles' heads poking out of the water, waiting for one of them to strike out. They were so close to their prey yet they didn't move.

The tourists grew impatient when it seemed as though nothing was going to happen and so the bus moved on again and headed round the west of the lake towards the exit of the valley and onto the great plains.

Just before they left the Umbolo Valley one of the tourists spotted an unusual sight.

'There's a leopard asleep on the floor over there,' he said, 'and it's surrounded by a herd of antelope. It looks like, well, it can't be right but it looks like they are nudging the leopard.'

The driver stopped so they could all take a look but the sound of the engine clanking had the antelope scattering in different directions.

'That would seem like silly behaviour for antelopes,' said the guide, 'considering they are number one prey for the leopard! Sometimes the heat and the landscape can play tricks on what we see out here.'

'Yes, I guess so,' said the man doubtfully.
They lingered for a moment to see if the leopard would wake up. When it didn't, the bus moved on and made its way out of the valley.

Chapter 2

The sun rose slowly above the horizon and cast its warm rays over the Umbolo Valley. A light wind blew down the gentle slopes rustling the tall grasses as it flowed between them. A low rumbling could be heard in the distance but soon the sound grew nearer. A bus packed full of tourists rolled up one side of a hill and then down, slowly into the valley.

The first to hear it was the bat-eared fox.
His oversized ears had been pointing at the crest of the hill, awaiting the first sound of the engine and now it was his job to let everyone else know it was coming.
'It's on its way!' he shouted.
'Everyone get ready! Get into position.'
The bat-eared fox raced on down the valley shouting his warning as he went by.
The bus wasn't far behind him but soon stopped when it spotted the lioness in

the long grass. She was busy stalking one of the wildebeest that had wandered off from the rest of the herd.

'Hey,' she whispered as she slowly crept closer. 'Are you new? I haven't seen you before,'
Without looking up, the wildebeest replied;

'Yes, this is my first time but I think I know what to do.'

'Don't worry.' she said. 'I'm sure you'll be fine. I'll talk you through it. I'm about ten steps away from you now, so you count down as I walk and then you start running when I am five steps away. Ok?'

'Ok,' said the wildebeest in a shaky voice and started to count. '10, 9, 8, 7 …'

'Don't be nervous,' she said, trying to keep him calm, 'it's going to be fine.'

'6, 5, 4…wait! Did you say 5 steps?' the wildebeest asked.

'Go! Run!' roared the lioness as she pounced towards him.

The wildebeest was just quick enough to get out of the way and once he found his legs, soon built up speed. The lioness followed swiftly and stayed just on his tail. She chased him for a short while in a straight line before she shouted.

'Turn right and take the chase as close to the bus as you can!' she instructed.

The wildebeest instantly turned and did as she said. They flew past the front of the bus to the opposite side, the lioness leaping at his rear, bundling them both into the long grass and out of view of the tourists.

'Are you ok?' she said gasping for breath.

'Yes, I'm fine, I'm fine. That was amazing! Wow, you're a real pro!' said the wildebeest excitedly.

'You did an excellent job too. Now look, we must stay low for a while until the bus moves on and then you can make your way back to your herd. Ok?'

'Ok!' said the wildebeest.

The bus continued down the track and stopped in sight of one of the larger umbrella trees in the Umbolo Valley, where the three ostrich sisters were resting under the canopy.
Two were pretending to be asleep and had their heads stuck in the ground, whereas the other was searching for bugs under the bark of the tree.

They were waiting for the leopard, who was late again. He should have been here by now, ready in position, stalking them from behind the tree and ready for a chase but he was nowhere to be seen.

As she carried on pecking at the bark, the ostrich heard something behind her. She turned to see the cobra unfurl from a nearby branch. She stared at him for a confused moment before asking;

'What are you doing here?'

'The leopard sssent me inssstead of himsssself,' the cobra said, through a

shower of saliva. As a black spitting cobra, he was unable to talk without spitting. The poor ostrich was standing a little too close and got a dollop of spit in her eye.
It began to sting straight away.
She panicked and began squawking and running frantically in circles.

While all this took place on the ground, high up in the tree tops the crane family were arguing amongst themselves.

'It's your turn - I went last time.' said the mother crane to the father crane.

'No, it's not me today, its time you had a go!" he replied.
The mother crane glared at her husband.

'I'm sure you said you would take the next three turns, and this is the third one.' she said.

'Ok, ok! But next time it's definitely you.' the father crane admitted defeat.
The mother crane nodded her head and winked at her two chicks as their father made his way slowly up to the highest branch at the top of the tree. He stuck one

of his wings high into the air just as a huge shadow moved across the sky and plucked him swiftly from his perch.

He was carried off in the tight grip of the eagle to a distant crop of trees where upon he was set down gently into the branches out of sight of the bus.

'Hey!' said the crane crossly.

'What?' said the eagle.

'You need to cut your talons. They were digging in my wing a bit – I feel as though I've lost a few feathers!'

'Sorry.' the eagle apologised.

Meanwhile, the bus was being entertained by a couple of hares who had taken it upon themselves to start chasing each other out in the open. They were tearing up and down the grass, jumping on one another and stomping their huge rear feet.

It was enough to bring out a very grumpy and tired looking mongoose from her burrow.

'Please will you keep the noise down! It's my day off today and I want to get some rest,' she squealed at them. The hares instantly stopped their games and the mongoose turned her attention to the ostrich who was still distressed.

'Excuse me! What's the matter with you?' she asked.

'The cobra!' she squawked. 'He spat in my eyes and it really hurt!'

'Does it hurt now?" asked the mongoose.

'Well, no. I guess not.' she said.

'Then stop running around like a lunatic!' shouted the mongoose before disappearing back down her burrow.

The ostrich skulked back toward the umbrella tree where her sisters still stood with their heads buried in the dirt. She approached the cobra who had not moved from his branch but this time she left a distance between them before she started to talk.

'What did you mean when you said the leopard sent you?' she asked.

'The leopard sssaid he wasss too tired to chasse you ossstrichesss today ssso he asssked me to fill in for him.' the cobra spat out.

'How were you going to chase us?' asked the ostrich.

'I hadn't figured that bit out yet.'

'Typical of that leopard.' complained the ostrich.

By now, the bus was down by the lake where the warthogs were messing about in the mud and pretending not to have seen the two crocodiles close by in the water. The crocodiles let their heads poke out of the water so that they could just be seen by the bus.

'Come on,' teased one of the warthogs, edging closer to the water. 'Go for me! I bet I can be out of your reach before you've even broken the surface. Come on, do it!'

The crocodiles didn't bother to respond and instead sunk their heads beneath the water.

'Boo! Boo!' said the warthogs.
The bus rolled on round the side of the lake and towards the valley exit.

As well as the crocodiles, the leopard was also having a lazy day and was falling asleep not far from the dirt track.

'It's ok,' he thought as he drifted off. 'I told the cobra to fill in for me today so I can carry on dozing.'
The herd of antelope came upon him and, realising he was asleep, started to panic.

'He's meant to be further up the valley chasing the ostriches isn't he?' one of them said.

'No, he is meant to be stalking the wildebeest!' said another.

'Either way, he shouldn't be asleep!' said a third.
They began to try and nudge him awake but he wouldn't wake up.

21

With their efforts to stir the lazy leopard, they didn't hear the bus coming down the road behind them. It was only when it stopped and made a clunking noise that they knew it was there at all. The whole herd ran off in different directions away from both the bus and the leopard.

The bus did not stop for long, carrying on down the dirt track and eventually out of the valley altogether.

Chapter 3

Sometime later, the leopard stretched out his legs and opened his mouth to let out a huge yawn. Then he opened his eyes slowly and stared straight up. He wasn't greeted by the big blue sky he'd expected to see but instead had at least a dozen different sets of eyes looking down at him.

They did not look like happy faces as he glanced round at the familiar, frowning expressions.

The lion and lioness were there, one of the three ostriches, the cobra, the bat-eared fox, a couple of warthogs, a few antelope and the crane family.

'Morning.' said the leopard as he got to his feet.

'Is that all you have to say?' demanded the lion.

'I think you have some explaining to do,' said the lioness.

'Do I?' the leopard yawned.

'Well, you do to me!' said the ostrich.

The leopard looked up at her and noticed her eyes were looking a bit red and sore.

'What happened to you?' he asked her.

'That wasss me.' said the cobra apologetically.

The ostrich explained what had happened under the umbrella tree. When she had finished, the leopard said;

'Well, what's the problem? You still put on quite a show by the sounds of it!'

The other animals did not look amused. One of the antelope went on to explain that they had come across him and, fearing he had overslept, tried to wake him.

'The bus almost caught us trying to rouse you!' she exclaimed.

The leopard said sorry but couldn't really see why he had too.

I arranged for cobra to take over my role so I could sleep a while. I thought it would be ok.' he said.

'You thought wrong!' roared the
lion. 'Your selfishness today got one of the
ostriches hurt and could have given the
whole game away.'

'This is why we have a set plan,' said
the lioness, 'so we can avoid situations
like this!'

'I'm really sorry,' said the leopard
and this time he meant it.

'I think we'd better have a meeting,'
the lion said. 'We need to remind
ourselves why we do this.'

The lion looked to the bat-eared fox
and asked him to spread the word that
there all the animals should gather down
by the lakeside later that day.

Before long, the animals began to
make their way to the lake.
When they were settled, the lion climbed
on top of a large rock. From this position
he could see everyone, even the flamingos
and crocodiles who preferred to stay
within the water.

'I have asked you all here today,' he started, 'to remind you why it is important for us to put on the show we do when the bus comes to the valley.

I know some of you will have heard this story many times before but there are some,' he paused a moment and looked over at some of the younger animals, 'for whom this will be the first time.

A long time ago, this valley was a completely different place. It looked the same but it was dangerous, a constant battle between life and death. It had been this way for generations - animals trying to survive and having to eat each other. But there was balance to it and it worked.

That was until the humans came.

The humans did not see how the valley functioned as a whole and removed what they wanted. They came and took some of the animals, mainly the bigger, stronger ones, away in big cages never to be seen again. Before long, the fragile balance of the valley had been lost.

My father and his generation knew something had to be done soon as some of them were down to just a few of their kind and if they disappeared, they would all be affected.

All the animals put aside their differences and came together to find a solution. They decided not to compete with or prey on each other and instead adapted. The meat eaters agreed to only eat the meat of those animals that had died naturally and added berries and fruits to their diets.

They worked together to show the humans that animals are of more value running free. They realised that part of the excitement for the humans was the thrill of watching the hunt so routines were set up between the remaining animals to entertain them.

These routines have been replayed a hundred times over since and so every time that bus shows up, we have to perform. If we don't, they'll get bored and take us away in their cages again.'

The lion paused and looked down at the leopard and then towards the crocodiles before carrying on,

"I know some of you are tired and don't see the point of what we do but if you need a reminder, simply look at the black rhino. He is the last of his kind for miles and miles round here. We could all end up on our own like him if we don't perform. It's only once every couple of days, so let's stick to our schedules and practice our routines.'

There was a murmur of agreement from all the animals.

On his way down from the rock, the lion was stopped by the bat-eared fox.

'When was the last time you saw the black rhino?' the bat-eared fox asked.

'I really don't know,' replied the lion. 'Why don't you and eagle go and see if you can find him?'

The bat-eared fox and the eagle had travelled quite far and crossed from their valley into the neighbouring one when the eagle spotted the black rhino high up on a ridge on a rocky outcrop.

'Surely there is nothing for him to eat up there,' said the bat-eared fox.

'Let's go and have closer look and see what he's up to,' said the eagle.
The eagle rose up in the air and made off in the direction of the ridge while the bat-eared fox climbed up the slope.
Both arrived at the same time and the black rhino did not look pleased to see either of them. He was a grump at the best of times but today he looked as if he was in a terrible mood.

'Leave me alone!' he snapped abruptly.

'We came to see if you are ok.' said the eagle gently.

'I am the biggest thing round here - I'm fine. Now clear off!'

'Wouldn't you rather come back to the Umbolo Valley and be amongst friends?' asked the bat-eared fox.

'Better than staying up here on your own,' added the eagle.

'I'm alone wherever I go. Leave me!' shouted the black rhino.
He was right when he said he was the biggest thing around. He may well have not been as quick as either of them but he could hurt them if he wanted to.

The bat-eared fox and the eagle took the hint and headed back home.

Chapter 4

All was well in the valley for a few weeks.
Buses came by every couple of days and all the animals knew and stuck to their schedules.

A few of them could rotate roles but the star attractions always needed to make an appearance. The eagle, the leopard and the lioness were the highlights for the tourists and were kept busy.
The lion also played his role, every now and again giving a brief glimpse of himself to the occasional bus, which would always rock excitedly at the sight of him.

One day the sun rose to a misty morning and the animals began to stir.

The lion woke to an unusual groaning noise beside him. He looked over his shoulder and at his wife who was rubbing her stomach.

'I think I ate too many figs yesterday. I have a terrible stomach ache.' she said. 'I don't think I can do it today.'

The lion looked at his wife concerned and offered to take her part.

'Don't be silly. Everyone knows that it's the female lion that hunts.' she said.

'Not in this valley.' he replied. 'It's neither of us!'

They both chuckled.

'Seriously, I'll go out and do it today.' insisted the lion. 'I've watched you a hundred times so I know how it's done.'

The lioness agreed and with that she shut her eyes and went back to sleep.

The lion made his way out from their lair and up the slope to where a wildebeest was waiting patiently.

'Morning!' said the lion cheerily.

The wildebeest looked up in shock as he saw the thick mane of the lion.

'Er…,' he hesitated. 'I'm waiting for the lioness?'

'She's not coming today. You're going to have to settle for me.'

'You?' puzzled the wildebeest. 'Do you even know how to?'

'I've watched my wife enough times. How tricky can it be?'
The wildebeest gulped as the lion made his way behind him and lay down in the grass.

'You'll have to move back further than that.' instructed the wildebeest.
The lion got up and started backing further away.

'Keep going, keep going,' said the wildebeest. 'Keep going. OK. Stop. Now crouch down. Lower, lower and tuck your tail in. Ok, that's fine, stay like that.'
The bat-eared fox came running past announcing the arrival of the bus and nearly tripped over when he spotted the lion lying in the grass.

'What are you doing?' he exclaimed.

'Taking my turn,' replied the lion. 'The lioness is not well.'

'Oh my! I do hope you know what you're doing!' he said before running on.

Moments later, the bus came up and over the hill and down towards where the wildebeest stood. Other than pretending to graze, he didn't move his head at all as he started to guide the lion in.

'Now begin by stalking towards me.' he whispered. 'Slowly does it. That's right, keep low and try not to make any noise.' The lion followed the instructions and slowing edged towards his target.

'Jump now! Pounce! Jump!' yelled the wildebeest as he turned to sprint away. The lion leapt into the air narrowly missing the back legs of the wildebeest as he sprinted off in a straight line. The wildebeest turned this way and that, leading the lion every which way.
They did two full circuits of the bus before the wildebeest led the lion into the long grass, diving in and out of sight. The lion had made the finish look as convincing as when the lioness did it.

They both lay in the grass in a bundle of legs and the lion started laughing excitedly.

'That was amazing! Wow!' said the lion. He looked over at the wildebeest. 'You're a real pro!'

'Good morning, ladies and gentlemen,' said the guide on the bus, 'and welcome to the Umbolo Valley safari adventure. Hopefully, this morning you will be able to see some of the wildlife that this country has to offer so keep your eyes peeled...'
The guide was halfway through his normal introduction speech when he looked out of the window. Instead of seeing the lioness stalking her prey as usual, he was looking at the male lion hunting.
'What... what...what?' he stuttered.
'Well I never. People, you are in for a real treat today. Driver, stop the bus!'
The tourists all stared out the window in the direction that the guide was looking.

'This is very unusual,' continued the guide, 'as it is normally the female lion that does the hunting. To see a male lion stalking its dinner is a very special sight. A very special sight indeed!'

The tourists all watched on as the lion crouched down close to the ground and edged closer and closer to his prey.

'This male lion seems to know what it is doing,' said the guide. 'See how he keeps his body low and keeps his tail tucked in and out of sight. This poor wildebeest has no idea of the danger approaching.'

The chase erupted in front of them as the lion sprung out from the grass and the wildebeest darted out of its way just in time. They ran all over and then straight towards the bus.

As the tourists ran from window to window to follow the action, the bus rocked from side to side. After two complete laps of the bus, the wildebeest ran into the long grass, the lion followed and they disappeared from view.

'Do you think he got him?' someone asked excitedly.

'Most likely.' said the guide and he went on to explain the significance of what they had just seen to the tourists. 'There could be a number of reasons for this strange behaviour from the male lion. Most likely is that the lioness is injured or maybe worse and so the lion must catch his own dinner. Normally there would be other female lions in the pride who could take over the role but this valley is quite unique, there are only the two lions. This is the first example of a male lion hunting I have ever come across. If he's done it today, I am sure he will hunt again.'

The bus engine started up again and continued with the rest of the safari.

Chapter 5

The animals had performed an outstanding show the previous day and today some were relaxing by the lake while others were off foraging for food.

Suddenly, the bat-eared fox came racing down the valley shouting.

'It's coming! It's coming! It's coming!'

The animals all looked up at once.

'Don't be silly,' yawned the lion, stretching as he got to his feet. 'It was here yesterday. You probably heard a rumble of thunder.'

'No, he's right dear,' said the lioness, as she came running down the valley in a panic. 'It's coming over that hill any second and nobody's ready! What we do?'

The lion looked around at all the animals gathered and then began to roar his instructions. He looked to the lioness first.

'Run towards the top of the valley and take one of the antelope with you.

Make the chase last as long as you can, so we have time to get things organised down here.'

An antelope volunteered and the lion made a point of looking at him.

'We're counting on you to buy us some time.' he said.

'I won't let you down.' said the antelope and set off with the lioness.

The lion turned his attention back to the others. He spotted the eagle perched in a nearby tree.

'Go and find the leopard and tell him to meet the ostriches under the umbrella tree for a chase.'

The eagle swiftly made off and the lion continued to shout instructions.

The flamingos were sent to find the crocodiles while the rest of the animals were arranging themselves further down the valley.

The lioness and the antelope were treating the bus to a real show. The chase was running circles around the bus and had been going on for quite some time.

'I'm getting cramps in my back legs!' yelled the antelope.

'Ok… we should… probably…. finish soon…' gasped the lioness.

'I'm going for the big finish.' said the antelope, turning for one final time and then running into the long grass.
The lioness followed and shoved him to the ground out of view.
They both lay there panting a while before the lioness finally spoke.

'I hope… we gave them all enough time.'
They had done a good job but just to be sure, the lion emerged from the long grass and paraded in front of the bus, holding the passengers' attention for as long as they were interested.

By the time the bus moved on, the rest of the animals were ready.

The leopard chased the ostrich, the eagle took the crane, the aardvark and the porcupine were out and even the mongoose was ready.

By the lake, the flamingos flocked together and the crocodiles feigned attacking the warthogs.

When the bus had left the valley, the animals gathered at the shore of the lake. Those who had taken part in the activities looked exhausted whilst everyone else looked confused.

'Well,' said the lioness, 'that was a little unexpected!'

'You can say that again.' said the lion.

'Why do you think it came today? Will there be another one tomorrow? Will there be one every day?' one of the ostriches was working herself into a frenzy. 'What are we to do? We can't do this every day. We won't have any energy left to gather food. We won't have any time!'

'Shut her up!' the lion roared at her sisters. 'I'm trying to think!'

The two ostriches gathered round their sibling who was wobbling from side to side with worry. They talked to her gently and eventually calmed her down.

The lion stood silent for a moment, staring at the bus kicking up dust as it wound its way in the distance.

'It's going to be alright.' he announced. 'I think this was a one off. There may be another bus tomorrow as normal but I don't think there will be one every day.'

The other animals seemed relieved at this news. They did not question how the lion knew it for which he was grateful as he was not so sure. This change in events could alter everything for them and he hoped it really was a one off.

Chapter 6

The following day brought another bus into their valley.

It had been expected and so the animals were organised and put on a convincing show.

What they weren't prepared for though, was another bus the following day.

And the day after that.

And every day for the rest of the week.

After the 5th day of shows, all the animals arranged a meeting at the lake. They were tired, they were hungry, they were confused, they were scared and they were all arguing with each other.

The lion climbed up onto the rock that stuck out into the lake and let out a terrifying roar that soon silenced all their quarrelling.

'Will you all just stop!'

The lion had all their attention in an instant.

'Look,' he started in a much quieter voice, 'I know it has been a difficult week for all of us. We are all exhausted. I'm as puzzled as you but arguing amongst ourselves is not going to help anything. We need to work together and figure out what we're going to do.'

'Why have things changed?' asked one of the ostriches.

'I don't know,' said the lion. 'As far back as I can remember there has only ever been a bus once every two days. Does anyone remember anything different like this before?'

'I do,' said a deep voice from the back of the group. 'I remember a time when there would have been two or three buses a day.'

All the animals turned around to see who was talking, then stepped aside one by one to let the black rhino walk between them.

'Nice to see you, black rhino.' the lion said smiling as he climbed down from the rock to greet him personally. 'Please, tell us what you know.'

The black rhino turned slowly to face the rest of the animals and cleared his throat.

'When I was a lot younger,' he started, 'I would spend most of my time down by this lake with my wife. The buses used to come as they do now. There would be one every couple of days and they would keep their distance from us. Some of your parents would have entertained them higher up the valley but it was here that the buses spent most of their time. They wouldn't bother us and we were happy for a time.

Ater a time, we wanted to start our own family. We had a beautiful baby girl and then that's when everything changed. For everybody.

The buses started to turn up every day. Sometimes up to three buses a day and we just couldn't keep up with them. We were exhausted having to perform so often and sometimes when they came, we would be resting or fast asleep. That was when the humans started to leave the buses. They would come closer to us and try to touch us.'

All of the animals gasped and started whispering amongst themselves before the black rhino carried on.

'One day in particular, a bus pulled up just over there.' he indicated the dirt track with his head and then turned to face the lake. 'A group of the humans walked out and came over to where my family and I were stood. They approached my daughter, they came too close and my wife got frightened. She ran over to scare them away. That was all she wanted to do - just scare them. But one of the humans fell over in front of her.'

He shook his head sadly.

'My wife she,' he hesitated, 'she couldn't stop in time and she trampled on it. She didn't mean to but it was too late. She must have hurt it quite badly as it had to be carried back onto the bus.

A few days went by and there was no sign of any buses.

Then it came but it wasn't the same. This bus had cages. It came straight down to the lake where we were and the humans got out. There were so many of them and they were all carrying weapons.'

The black rhino paused and from where he was, the lion could see the tears forming in his eyes. The black rhino took a deep breath, turned to face the animals once more and continued.

'The humans surrounded us from all sides and started shooting. I took a few shots to my body and one close to my head which was enough to knock me unconscious for a time. When I came round, the humans were gone.
The bus was gone.
My family, my family were gone.

It was our beautiful baby rhino that made them come more frequently. For you now, something must have changed, something unusual that they want to see more often.'

The animals looked around at each other but it was the leopard who said it.

'You!' he said accusingly, pointing at the lion. 'You did this!'

'What? Why me?' protested the lion.

'It's ever since you did your chase. That's when the buses started to come every day. They want to see a male lion hunting.' the leopard said.

'That's not fair!" defended the lioness 'He was covering for me because I was unwell.'

All the animals started to bicker again.

'Ok, ok. Calm down. Pointing pawsss, hoovesss and wingsss at each other won't help anything.' the soothing voice of the cobra cut through the noise. 'The way I sssee it, we're better off working together rather than againssst each other.' The cobra slid his way to the front of the group. 'We'll have to carry on asss we have been and make do asss bessst we can. Thossse of usss who can ssswap rolesss ssshould do ssso asss often as posssible. The rest of usss ssshould make oursssselvesss asss ussseful asss possible.'

'He's right.' agreed the black rhino. 'Now is not the time to mess this up. You don't want to end up like me.'
The animals visibly shook at the prospect and those with children held them closer.

'Are you going to ssstick around?' the cobra asked the black rhino.
The black rhino stared out and caught the eyes of the bat-eared fox.

'You're amongst friends here.' said the bat-eared fox.
The black rhino nodded slowly and smiled.

The following days were difficult but the animals struggled through. Those taking part in the daily performances were looking increasingly tired and those not directly involved were kept busy foraging for fruit and berries for everyone else.

The black rhino was helping by positioning himself in full view down by the lake side. It was difficult for him to reprise his role but he did and everyone was grateful for the attention he grabbed.

Additional help also came from the baboon family who had always kept a distance but agreed to move their home to a tree closer to the dirt track. This was a big attraction for the buses and they often hovered for lengthy periods watching the family swing around the massive canopy and then chase each other on the ground. The baboon children were bold and inquisitive and even after repeated warnings from their parents, began to venture closer and closer to the stationary buses.

One day, when a young male baboon had ignored his parents' warnings again, he found himself within touching distance of the bus. Whilst sitting on the ground looking at the many faces staring back at him, he heard a loud hissing noise and then the door opened.

The young baboon jumped back in fright but then his curiosity got the better of him. He approached cautiously.

One of the humans was leaving the bus.

'Son!' his father yelled over to him. 'Come here son! Don't go anywhere near it!'

The young baboon ignored the cries of his father and stared at the human in front of him. It had something in its hand and it smelled amazing. He edged closer to the human who was waving the object in his direction.

'Don't you dare go any closer!' screeched his mother but again the young baboon ignored her. The mother baboon looked at the father baboon pleading with him to do something. The father baboon hesitated before running in his son's direction but he was too late.

The youngster was close enough to snatch the offered item just before he was bundled out of the way by his father. He shook off his father's grip and climbed to the very top of the umbrella tree in amongst the spindly branches where he knew he could not be got at.

'Don't you dare eat that!' his father shouted up to him.
But he had already bitten off a massive chunk of the brown, sticky, sweet tasting food. His eyes lit up and he nearly fell clean off the branch he was sat on.

'Wow! What a taste,' he thought. He gobbled up the rest of it and only then made his way back down the tree where his mother, father and younger sister were scowling.

'Didn't you hear me?' asked his father. 'I told you not to eat that.'

'And I told you to stay away from the bus.' his mother scolded.

'And I want to know why you didn't save any of that smelly stuff for me?' his sister said angrily.

Both the mother and father baboon continued to shriek wildly at their son for disobeying them but the young male wasn't paying any attention. He was too busy distracted by the amazing taste still in his mouth.

Meanwhile the human had been joined by two others and they were slowly moving in the direction of the baboon family.

By the time the parent baboons turned around, they had three large humans looming over them. The baboons squealed in surprise and scattered.

The humans stood and watched the alarmed animals run off and so looked for something else.

The aardvark, oblivious to everything going on around him, had his head deep in an ants' nest. He was busy munching on a particularly crunchy ant when he felt something strange and warm on his back. He pulled his head out of the dirt and spotted the porcupine standing nearby.

He looked shocked.

The aardvark peered over his shoulder to the source of the strange sensation.

It was a human hand.

'It's touching me.' said the aardvark in a surprisingly calm voice.

'It's touching you.' echoed the porcupine.

'What do I do?' asked the aardvark.

'Don't do anything.' suggested the porcupine. 'Maybe it'll stop.'

The aardvark stayed perfectly still. The hand didn't move and then the human made a noise.

The aardvark noticed the porcupine's eyes widen before he felt the second hand.

'Now there two of them. Both touching me.' the aardvark said, this time a little less calmly.

'They're both touching you!' agreed the porcupine.

'What do I do now?' he asked.

The second human also made a noise.

'There's another one coming over!' the porcupine said alarmed.

Before the third human got any closer, the aardvark shrugged them off and shuffled forwards. He quickly disappeared into a dense shrub and hid.

The humans turned their attentions to the porcupine.

'No chance!' grunted the porcupine and he raised his quills.

The humans immediately backed off, got back on the bus and it drove away.

Three humans had left the bus and only wandered around for a moment but they had left behind a visibly shaken aardvark and a baboon with a taste for chocolate.

Chapter 7

Things became even more complicated and stressful for the animals when two buses began to turn up each day. The animals were exhausted and they started making mistakes.

One morning the lioness was nearing the end of her morning chase. The antelope turned, ran round the bus and towards the long grass for the finish. The lioness was at full speed when she stumbled and ended up colliding into the back of the antelope. The two of them fell to the ground and lay there for a few moments, both a little dazed.
The antelope rolled onto her side panting and as she did, she saw dozens of beady little eyes staring down from the bus with their mouths wide open.

'Pssst!' the antelope made a noise from the corner of her mouth to get the lioness's attention. 'They're all looking at us.' she whispered.

'Oh,' said the lioness noticing.

'Quick - grab me by the leg!' ordered the antelope.

'What?' said the lioness.

'Grab me by the leg!' the antelope said urgently. 'Grab me and drag me into the grass.'

The lioness got to her feet and stuck out a paw in the direction of the antelope.

'No!' yelped the antelope. 'You need to make it look like you got me. Use your mouth.'

'My mouth? But I ...'

'Just do it! And try and be gentle,' said the antelope.

The lioness looked up at the bus. All the eyes were on her. She had never felt so nervous but she put her head down, opened her jaw wide and clamped her mouth around the antelope's leg.

'Ow! Ow! Not so hard! Ow!' squealed the antelope.

It took the lioness some time to drag the antelope out of sight of the bus but eventually, when they could no longer be seen, she let go.

'Ouch!' the antelope got up and was limping around.

'I'm really sorry. I guess I don't know my own strength.' said the lioness.

'No, it's fine. A few days and I should be able to walk again.' The antelope said as she hobbled away. 'That was too close though, too close...'

Some of the other animals were not at the top of their game either.
The leopard was busy stalking the three ostriches, two of whom had their heads stuck firmly in the ground as normal. The only problem was that instead of just pretending, they were sound asleep. The third ostrich was desperately trying to wake them but with no success. Before she knew it, the leopard was almost on top of her and she had to start running. She was not used to being chased on her own and found that she did not really know how to

perform without the aid of her sisters. She was growing increasingly frantic as the leopard first complained that she was going too fast, and then she was going too slowly.

'Quicker!' he shouted.

'What?' said the ostrich. 'I can't hear you.'

'Run quicker!' repeated the leopard.

'What?' again she couldn't hear what he was saying. She turned her head around to look back at him.

'Don't look at me!' yelled the leopard. 'Look where you're going!'
It was too late.
She ran straight into one of the lower branches of the umbrella tree and knocked herself out.
The leopard came to a complete stop and just stared at her lying on the ground. He didn't know what to do so he just stood there looking at her. Normally they would either run into the distance and out of the way or he would pretend to give up and

just walk away. He was never supposed to catch up. He looked down at the ostrich lying on the ground, looked up at the bus and then came to a decision.
He ran off.
Away from the stricken ostrich, away from the bus; he ran and he didn't stop.

The bus door opened again and this time, nearly all the humans got out.
The two ostrich sisters still had their heads firmly in the ground and had no idea of the imminent danger to them or their sister.
The porcupine and the cobra were nearby as they spotted the humans approach their vulnerable friends.
There was one more animal too - the young male baboon. He was brazenly moving towards the crowd of humans. His eyes were fixed on one in particular. He could smell it in on them, that tempting scent of chocolate.
He ran straight to the feet of the human and the rest of them paused at his

approach. All manner of noises came from the crowd but he paid no attention. He also ignored the yells and shouts of his parents from way behind; his eyes were fixed on the human's pocket.

He suddenly leapt up and climbed the human's leg.

The human starting wriggling and trying to shake him off but the baboon was quick. He thrust his hand into the pouch and pulled out the chocolate and ran off. He raced to the top again and after a few moments of nibbling and gnawing, he finally had the skin off and sunk his teeth into the sticky, sweet block. This one was bigger than before but in no time, he'd scoffed the lot.

He had the wonderful taste again but a few moments later his stomach ached and he felt sick.

His father climbed up and carefully picked up his son. When they reached the ground, the young baboon looked very sorry for himself as he looked up at his mother.

'I'm sorry mum,' he sobbed. 'I won't do it again.'

After the distraction of the baboon's thievery, the humans were making their way over to the stricken ostrich.
The porcupine and the cobra moved closer too.
'What do we do?' asked the worried porcupine.
'We can't leave her.' said the cobra. 'They might hurt her - or worssse!'
The crowd edged closer.
The porcupine raised his quills threateningly and snorted angrily.
Some of the humans stopped but the rest were still curious enough to come closer.
The cobra coiled himself on the floor and raised his head and neck up proudly. He pointed himself in the direction of the nearest human.
'Ssso what now?' he asked the porcupine, but it was too late. He spat as he spoke and it landed right in the eyes of

the human. Its arms went straight to its face and it started to make a high-pitched squealing noise.

Another human picked a stick up but before it could even begin to swing it in anger at the cobra, the porcupine moved between them, brushing his quills against the human's legs. They stuck in easily and it too started scream as it backed away. The other humans helped their friends back to the bus and it left.

The bus didn't make its way down to the lake as usual but instead turned around and went back up the dirt track the way they had come in.

'Oh no,' said the cobra. 'What have we done?'

'You did the same thing any of us would have done,' said a voice from behind him. The lion was walking over. 'I saw what you did to protect the ostrich and it was very brave.'

'But now they are going to come back, like black rhino told us,' said the porcupine nervously, 'and take us away.'

Chapter 8

As word spread of what had happened, none of the animals blamed the porcupine or the cobra for their actions. The ostrich sisters, once they had all woken up, were beyond grateful for what they had done. However, everybody was scared about what would happen next.

The black rhino was the first to address them.

'You all know what happened to my family. I fear this time they will come after you two.'

He looked down at the porcupine and the cobra who both looked terrified.

'If they come after our friends, they will have to deal with the rest of us too!" declared the aardvark, sounding braver than he felt.

The other animals all cheered and shouted in agreement.

'We have to come up with a plan, a way of protecting not just two of us, but all of us.' suggested the lioness.

The animals spent much of the rest of the day discussing what they should do next and devised a whole new performance. Just as in the black rhino's tale, there was no bus the following day which allowed them all to both rest and perfect their roles.

It was three days until the familiar rumbling sound could be heard.
As usual, the bat-eared fox was the first to hear it coming and he was quick to act. He waited until the bus reached the very crest of the hill in front of him to confirm it was what he expected. Just as black rhino had said, not the regular bus but a hunter's bus. The bat-eared fox turned and made his way down the dirt track as normal, announcing the arrival as he went.

'It's coming. Everybody ready! The hunters' bus is coming down behind me!'

Everybody was ready.

Everybody was in position.

The hunters came down the track at quite a pace and first to strike were the baboons. The family were hiding either side of the dirt track in amongst the low shrubs.

As the bus approached, they each in turn sprang up, took aim and threw small rocks. Most of them bounced off the hard side of the bus but a few struck against the windows and smashed holes in the glass. From up above a shadow moved across the sky. It was the eagle and he had the cobra dangling from his talons. He flew over the roof of the bus, which had reduced its speed under attack, and dropped the cobra on its top.

The cobra's scaly skin stuck fast to the bus roof and he was able to make his way to the edge. He peered over the side and spotted one of the holes the baboons had made. He dangled down and quickly slid through and inside. He got down to the floor without being seen by any of its occupants who were all gathered near to the front. He peered around to see if he could see any cages but there were none. There were only weapons, some of which he recognised from black rhinos' description of them.

'I sssupossse I had better make my presssence known,' he said to himself. He slithered towards the humans. It was difficult to tell how many there were but his instructions were clear; to take out as many as he could.

He wound up a metal leg and onto a seat. From this position it was easier to attack but first he had to get their attention.

'Excussse me!' he hissed loudly. The two nearest both turned around to see what the noise was and got fresh, stinging spit in their faces for their trouble. They began screaming and rubbing their hands at their eyes.

'I wouldn't do that,' hissed the cobra with a grin on his face. 'you'll only make it worssse!'

The screams got the attention of the rest of the humans including, it would appear, the driver, because as he turned round, the bus violently jerked to one side.

This presented the cobra with another target as the human was propelled over his screaming friends and left lying on his back, looking straight up at the cobra.

'Pleasssed to meet you!' the cobra said, spitting into his face too.

More screaming erupted by which time the other humans had figured out what was striking their friends down. A few of them started making their way towards him, shielding their faces with their hats, their clothes or just their hands.

'Now that'sss cheating,' hissed the cobra, annoyed and he slunk back down towards the floor. 'I think it'sss time I left!'

He hurried to the back of the bus back and out through another hole.

When he emerged, he was greeted by one of the ostriches running alongside the bus. She grabbed him with her beak and pulled him from danger just as a human made a grab for his tail.

The bus carried on down the valley but at a reduced speed and came to a complete stop not far from the umbrella tree. Immediately, the door opened and the hunters jumped out, three of their number with red, sore looking eyes.

The porcupine was not far away, apparently completely unaware that he had company. He had his back to them, his spines in a relaxed position and he was concentrating hard on which blade of grass he was going to chew on next. One of the hunters broke off from the pack and, slightly crouched to the ground, carrying a net, began to sneak up behind the porcupine.

The father crane was watching from the tree top above.

'He's about 10 steps away from you,' the crane squawked quietly.
The porcupine readied himself.
The hunter edged slowly forwards, staying close to the ground and trying to make as little noise as possible. He was within a few feet of the porcupine when the crane raised his warning.
By the time the hunter figured out that the squawking was giving him away, it was too late.
The porcupine quickly shuffled backwards into the hunters' legs and left half a dozen quills in his shins. The hunter fell and as it tried to get to his feet, rolled overexposing his bottom which the porcupine obligingly stabbed with a few more quills.
Once on his feet, the hunter rushed straight past his friends and back onto the bus.

The porcupine disappeared into the undergrowth.

The hunters spread out, each of them holding a different weapon. They began to beat at the low shrubs with sticks in an effort to flush the porcupine out but they were about to be greeted by something else entirely.

As one of them swung at a low bush, an orangey, brown blur burst out of nowhere and knocked him off his feet.

The hunter looked around dazed.

He could not work out what had hit him or where it had come from.

Two other hunters turned to assist but again, a blur of orange rammed their legs and had them falling to the ground.

The rest of the hunters took one glance at their fallen comrades and started retreating, their eyes looking every which way as they tried to figure out what was happening.

Once back on the bus, they swung around and went back the way they'd come.

'Good job guys. You can come out now. They've gone,' said the porcupine who crept out from behind a rock.
Slowly, the orangey brown blurs revealed themselves. It was the warthogs.
They had dug shallow holes to hide in and, once the humans had separated, they were easy targets for the speedy animals to tackle.

The bus steadily made its way up the dirt track out of the valley without knowing the animals had been busy.

The black rhino had put his strength to good use by moving huge boulders across the track along with some debris from a nearby tree. The hunters would be forced to stop and move the debris out of the way to get out of the valley.

The bat-eared fox was following the bus, observing it all the time. He carried on watching it as it began to slow down and come to a stop. It wasn't at the roadblock yet, so what were they doing?

He continued to watch as a few of the hunters got off and turned their attention to him. He was far enough for it to not be a problem though.

Until he noticed one had a weapon pointed at him.

There was a loud bang, and he felt an immense pain in his front right leg. He fell to the ground in agony.

The hunters were making their way towards him.

The bat-eared fox tried to move but it was too painful. He felt suddenly fearful as he realised, he was all alone. There wasn't anyone near enough to help him. He started to whimper as the hunter that had wounded him came closer and stood over him with his weapon pointed down.

The bat-eared fox had never been so scared and shut his eyes tightly for what would surely come next.

Suddenly, there was a snarl and then the hunter started yelling.

The bat-eared fox opened his eyes and saw the leopard with the hunter's arm in his mouth. He grappled with it for a couple of moments until it dropped its weapon.
The leopard stood between the bat-eared fox and the hunter, growling loudly.
Now it was the human who was now making the whimpering sounds.

'Can you move?' asked the leopard without turning.

'I think so,' replied the bat-eared fox.

'Then get yourself out of here.' ordered the leopard. 'Quick!'
The bat-eared fox knew that there was no time to hang around. He struggled to his feet and limped off down the valley towards the lake.
The leopard meanwhile stood his ground until he could see the bat-eared fox was out of danger.

'Now what do I do?' he thought to himself.
The hunter he had bitten was gone but some of the others were arranging

themselves in very threatening positions around him.

'I'm not running away this time,' he said under his breath. He growled at each hunter in turn as they circled around him.

Suddenly, there was a rumbling noise coming from the bottom of the valley, loud enough to distract both the leopard and the hunters.

They all looked toward a large haze of dust approaching fast.

It took a while to work out what it was but eventually the leopard could make out the herds of both the antelope and wildebeest joined by the warthogs. The cranes and the eagle were flying overhead and the leopard knew that the baboons and the porcupine would probably not be far behind.

The hunters found themselves once again retreating to the bus.

The herd stopped their charge when they could see the bus move off and the leopard went across to join them.

'I'm happy to see you,' he said.

'We heard the loud noise and guessed one of us was in trouble.' said the eagle.

The bat-eared fox got a wounded leg but I think he's ok. He headed down towards the lake.' said the leopard.

'Can you go see that he made it ok?' the eagle asked the cranes.
The cranes had had the same idea and were mid-take off before the eagle even finished his sentence.

'That was a brave thing you did, standing up to that many humans at once.' said one of the warthogs.
The rest of the animals murmured their agreement.

'Well,' said the leopard, 'we have to stick together don't we. Now let's finish it!'
With that, they were off and chasing the bus up the valley.

The bus was way ahead and just approaching the block in the road where it had to stop.

There were a couple of moments when nothing happened.

Then the door hissed opened and a couple of nervous looking hunters got off. They started moving some of the lighter tree debris out of the way but had to shout for the others to come help. Three more joined them and together they tried to lift one of the bigger logs in the road.

They had the shock of their lives when the log suddenly came to life.

A huge mouth opened very wide, revealing rows of sharp teeth and hissing in anger. Another log moved, a long, scaly tail that knocked one of the hunters over. Terrified and leaving their stricken friend on the floor, the other hunters fled back to the bus again.

The crocodiles grinned at each other and began walking towards the hunter who was lying face down to the ground obviously too scared to move.

'Wait!' a voice commanded. 'This one's mine!'

The hunter lay on the ground trembling nervously but he dared not move. He had seen a brief glimpse of the hungry mouth of the crocodile and he knew it wasn't far away. He had no idea what was going to happen next.
He had thought that this was going to be easy.
They had had strict instructions to drive down the Umbolo Valley and bring back a porcupine and a black spitting cobra which had both viciously attacked a tourist a few days before.
Things had not gone to plan though.
First the bus was attacked by baboons throwing rocks. Then the spitting cobra had somehow got onto the bus and spat its stinging venom into his friends' eyes. Since then, they had been charged by warthogs,

*pricked by a porcupine, bitten by a
leopard and now he was floored by a
crocodile.*

*'What next?' he thought as he lay
there frightened.*
*There was a sudden cold feeling on his
back. It was cold and it was strange.*
*He raised his head slightly and he could
see the windows of the bus where his
friends were staring wide eyed down at
him. They looked bewildered and their
expressions only scared him further. He
felt another cold sensation on his back and
he tried to turn his head around to look
behind him.*
There was an aardvark on his back.
An aardvark.
*He'd expected to see a crocodile or the
leopard but certainly not an aardvark. It
just stood there, grunting loudly.*

'Not pleasant, is it?' the aardvark
asked angrily. 'Not very nice being
touched by a strange creature, is it?'

'You'd better let him go back to his friends,' suggested one of the crocodiles. 'I think he's been scared enough.'
The aardvark reluctantly got down off the human and walked away.
The hunter got to his feet warily, ran towards the bus and climbed aboard.
There was nowhere for the bus to go though, the road was still blocked and the herds were approaching from behind.

The animals organised themselves as they surrounded the stricken bus. They could all see the bewildered hunters, their faces pressed up against the windows staring out.
The animals then closed in from all sides and when they were within a couple of metres, they stopped and stood perfectly still.

'Right,' the lion roared. 'Let's show these humans what we CAN do!'
The lion and lioness and the leopard roared. The cobra hissed, the baboons howled, the black rhino snorted loudly and

the warthogs and the aardvark grunted. The mongoose squeaked, the cranes and ostriches squawked, whilst the wildebeest and antelope stomped their hooves and the crocodiles opened their mouths wide to show off their teeth.

They kept the ruckus up for several moments, watching the hunters terrified faces.

Eventually, they fell silent.

The lion addressed the animals again;

'Now, let's show these humans what we WILL do!'

He walked to the front of the bus and the rest of the animals followed. They headed towards the debris in the road. The black rhino started to roll one of the bigger boulders out of the way, whilst some of the smaller animals were working together to move the tree branches. All the animals were helping move the obstruction out the way of the bus and before long the dirt track was clear again.

When they were done, the animals walked back past the bus making sure the hunters could see them leaving silently. The lion and the black rhino remained behind. The two of them stood at the front, staring down the driver and the hunters all looking back at them.

'What do you think will happen now? asked the lion.

The black rhino looked long and hard at the faces on the bus before he replied.

'I think they will leave us alone now.'

They parted, leaving the way clear.

The bus started up its engine and quickly drove away out of the valley.

It had been a couple of weeks and there had been no sign of any buses to the Umbolo valley. The animals were enjoying themselves and had lots more time to forage for berries and fruit and even more time to rest and relax.

The bat-eared fox had made a full recovery and the black rhino had stayed in the valley.

He was down by the lake talking to the lion.

'I think it is time for me to go.' the black rhino said.

'Oh,' said the lion. 'I thought you were going to stay with us?'

'I'd like to,' said the black rhino, 'but it really is time for me to move on.'

'We'll all miss you,' said the lion. 'We couldn't have done any of this without you. Be safe and know that you will always have friends in this valley.'

'Thank you.' said the black rhino. He made his way down the side of the lake and out the valley.

He walked for many days, sleeping for only short periods and eating food when he came across it. Eventually he climbed up and over the crest of a hill and found himself in a new valley he had not seen before. Looking around, he could see a small stream flowing into a large lake, umbrella trees dotted on the hillsides and many different animals either resting or playing.

A small head popped out from behind a low shrub nearby.

'Hello mate,' said the jackal. 'Are you lost?'

'What valley is this?' asked the black rhino.

'This is the Imroko Valley mate. And... oh no, not again. Not twice in one day!' the jackal was clearly alarmed as he looked beyond the black rhino. 'You'd better stay out of the way mate! It's coming!' He was off and running down the valley. 'It's coming, it's coming!"

The black rhino had just enough time to sink down in the long grass before a bus packed full of humans came over the hill and into the valley.

The black rhino could still hear the jackal shouting in the distance as he said to himself;
    'Here we go again!'

The end

Printed in Great Britain
by Amazon

41973188R00056